CHRISTMAS AT THE CABIN

A HEALING HEARTS SHORT STORY

LAURA FARR

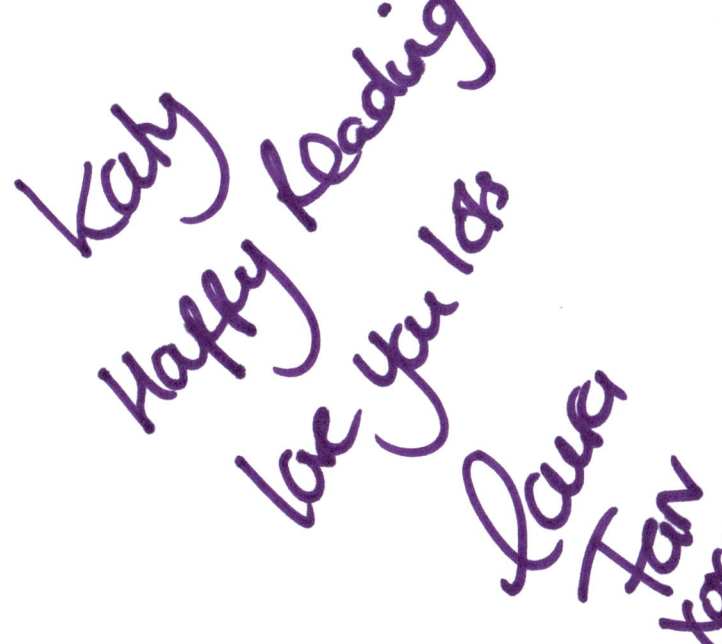

Katy

Happy Reading

love you lots

Laura

Farr

xoxo

CHAPTER ONE

Mason

"*L*ibby, sweetheart, it's a few nights away. You don't have to pack your whole closet," I shout as I take the stairs two at a time. Swinging open the bedroom door I see Libby leaning over the bed, frantically searching through a mountain of clothes.

"But you won't tell me where we're going. How can I pack when I don't know where we're going?" she pouts, her hands going to her hips as she turns to face me. "Can you at least give me a hint?"

I grin and make my way across the room, my eyes never leaving hers. She bites down on her lip and I feel my cock stir as my eyes linger on her gorgeous mouth.

Coming to stand in front of her, I wrap my arms around her waist and drop my lips to hers, kissing her gently.

"What if I told you that I plan on keeping you naked for the whole time and clothes won't be necessary," I mutter against her mouth before kissing her harder. Her hands reach up and slide around my neck. Her fingers tug on the hair at the base of my neck as I brush my tongue against her bottom lip, gaining entry into her mouth. She moans and the sound is like a direct line to my aching cock. Pulling out of the kiss, I scoop her up and toss her onto the pile of crumpled clothes on the bed.

"What are you doing?" she whispers as I stalk up the bed towards her, my hands coming to rest on either side of her head.

"Making love to my wife," I tell her, chuckling as her cheeks flush pink. We've been married for almost three years, but I can still make her blush as easily today as I could the day we met.

"I thought we had to leave?" she asks quietly, her eyes sparkling with desire.

"I think we have a little time," I murmur as I brush my lips against hers. My fingers trace under her top, causing her body to shiver at my touch. Pushing down the material of her bra I roll her nipple between my fingers, and her back arches in pleasure. Releasing her nipple, I quickly remove the bra and top she's wearing, sliding her jeans and panties off. My eyes sweep over her perfect, naked body and I smile as her face and neck flush a deeper shade of pink. As I pull my t-shirt over my head she sits up on her elbows, watching me hungrily while I slowly strip for her.

"Like what you see Mrs Walker?" I growl, running my hands up her bare thighs. Before she can answer me, I run my fingers through her wet folds, gently pushing one finger inside her. She gasps and squirms on the bed. "I'll take that as a yes, baby," I tell her as I lower my head between her legs, my tongue circling her clit as I push another finger inside.

"Oh my God Mason!" she cries. "Don't stop!"

I don't plan on it until she's begging me to. My fingers pump in and out of her while my tongue works over her clit. I know she's close as her breathing is labored and she's tugging on my hair. Reaching my hand up to her breast, I flick her nipple pushing her over the edge. Her legs lock around my head, as my name falls from her lips in a cry. My fingers and tongue keep up their assault as I tease the last of her orgasm from her body. Her legs finally relax, dropping their death grip on my head. She tries to move up the bed in an attempt to get away from my fingers and mouth. Chuckling against her I gently remove my fingers, licking them clean. I kiss my way up her body until I reach her mouth, capturing my lips with hers. She returns my kiss while gently pushing my shoulder, forcing me to lay on my back.

"What are you doing, baby?" I ask, knowing that she loves to be on top. Grinning, she straddles my hips before sinking down onto my hard length. I suck my breath in sharply as her warm heat envelops my cock. She throws her head back and moans. My fingers dig into the soft skin of her hips as I will her to move.

"Feel good?" she asks, and I nod as she begins to rock backwards and forwards.

"You feel amazing Lib." She drops her head to mine and kisses me, snaking her tongue into my mouth.

"You feel pretty good, too," she whispers and I growl flipping her onto her back, needing to be in control. She squeals at the sudden movement and I waste no time pushing back inside her, holding her legs as I pound into her body. Leaning down I take one of her nipples into my mouth. A loud moan falls from her lips as my tongue circles around her nipple. Her hands rake over my back, as her nails scratch my skin. She's close again and I'm right there with her. Releasing her nipple with a pop, I kiss up her neck and look her straight in the eye.

"Come for me Libby," I demand. I thrust once more and she falls apart beneath me, her body shuddering with pleasure. Her release triggers my own and I groan into her neck, as my body covers hers. Kissing her softly on the jaw, I roll to the side and she wraps herself around me.

"Wow!" she exclaims. "Maybe we should just stay here and do that for the next three days!" Her voice is tinged with amusement, but I think she might be serious.

I laugh and roll her on to her back. "I can promise plenty more of that Mrs Walker," I say kissing her gently. Climbing off the bed I start putting my clothes back on. "Come on, let's get going."

"But I still haven't packed."

"I told you, no clothes required," I say with a wink, laughing as she rolls her eyes at me before tossing the pillow at my head.

CHAPTER TWO

Libby

"So where are we going?" I ask Mason excitedly as he puts two overnight bags in the back of the truck. Despite his insistence that I didn't need clothes, I'd thrown some outfits in a bag, along with Mason's Christmas presents. He surprised me earlier in the week, telling me we were going away for Christmas, as well as celebrating our third wedding anniversary. A break away was just what we needed, the past twelve months had been tough. I'd finished my last year of University and had been trying to get a job ever since. I was helping out on my Aunt and Uncle's ranch until I could find something, but it wasn't ideal.

"You'll have to wait and see, baby," Mason says with

a wink as he reaches around me and opens the truck door. I pout and he chuckles before kissing me quickly on the lips. "Hop in. You won't have to wait too long, it's only about a forty five minute drive." Grinning, I do as he says and watch as he walks around the front of the truck and climbs into the driver's seat.

Thirty minutes later and I'm bouncing in my seat as we pass the second road sign for Lake Buchanan. We visited the lake last summer with my cousin Savannah and her family, and I loved it there. I'm excited to know if that's where we were headed.

"Are we going to Lake Buchanan?" I ask turning in my seat to face Mason. His lips turn up in a smile and he slowly turns his head.

"Yes sweetheart, we're going to Lake Buchanan. Now stop asking questions, I'm not telling you anything else." He winks at me and turns back to face the road. I grin and gaze out of the window at the passing scenery, the edge of the lake just coming into view.

Ten minutes later and Mason is pulling off the main road and turning down a bumpy dirt track. Dense trees line the track as far as the eye can see and the track looks as if it hasn't been used in years. I squeal and hold onto my seat as the truck hits a pot hole and lurches to the right. The truck groans and Mason's hand finds my thigh, squeezing gently.

"You okay, sweetheart?" he asks, his voice tinged with amusement.

"I'm fine," I scoff. "Are you sure this is the right way? It doesn't look like anyone's driven down here in forever."

"Yep!" he exclaims. "Look." He points in front of him just as the dirt track opens wide to reveal a beautiful log cabin.

"Mason, this is amazing," I gush, my eyes darting around to take everything in. The cabin is surrounded by trees and a small picnic table sits off to one side. The cabin isn't huge, but it looks perfect for just the two of us. There is a large covered porch with a swing, and as I peer between the trees, I can spot the lake only a few hundred yards from the cabin. The trees surrounding the cabin make it completely private and essentially hidden away.

"Merry Christmas baby," he says quietly and I turn to see him watching me, a huge smile on his face.

"Merry Christmas," I tell him before launching myself across the cab and into his arms. Laughing he moves his seat back to accommodate me and I straddle his lap, his erection hard between my legs. As his arms wrap around me he bends his head, kissing me urgently. I grind my hips into him and he growls into my mouth.

"You need to stop sweetheart, or else I'll be fucking you in this truck," he warns, his voice low.

"I wouldn't say no to that," I mutter against his lips. Reaching my hands under his t-shirt, I brush my fingers along his abs. His hands wrap around my wrists and he stops my groping.

"As good as that sounds, let's get inside. I want you to see the cabin."

"Spoilsport," I tease, pecking him on the lips before wiggling in his lap one last time. Jumping from the truck I laugh as I hear Mason groan behind me.

Looking around I pull my jacket around my shoulders, the cold wind is a shock after the warmth of the truck. I feel Mason behind me and he pulls me back into his warm chest, his chin resting on my shoulder. "Shall we go inside?" he whispers in my ear. I nod and he takes my hand, guiding me towards the porch steps.

At the top of the steps I pause. "Is that a hot tub?" I squeal, looking over at the covered tub in the corner.

"It is," Mason confirms, smiling at my excitement.

"But I didn't bring a bikini," I tell him.

"Damn! Did I forget to tell you to bring one? Looks like you'll have to go in there naked then," he says flippantly and I smack him lightly on his shoulder.

"You never intended to tell me to bring a bikini, did you?" I ask with a laugh.

"I told you clothes weren't necessary." He shrugs tugging me away from the hot tub towards the door to the cabin. Reaching above the door frame he pulls down a key and quickly unlocks the door, pushing it open. I follow him in and gasp as he flicks on the lights. The door opens straight into a large living space. A comfy looking sofa sits on a shaggy rug in front of a huge fireplace. A small kitchen fills the back wall, creating an open plan room. Wooden stairs are off to the right, leading to what looks like an upstairs sleeping loft. To the left there are two doors, one to the bathroom which I can see as the door is slightly ajar, and another door which I assume leads to another bedroom. Looking up there are hundreds of fairy lights strung from the ceiling as well as winding up the staircase, and the floor is scattered with rose petals.

"Mason," I whisper. "This is beautiful. How did you arrange all of this?" I ask him in awe. Walking further into the room I spin around to take it all in, dragging my hand over the soft material of the sofa.

"Turns out the owner is an old romantic. When I told him what I wanted to do, he let me come over a few days ago and set everything up."

"Thank you," I tell him, reaching up to kiss him. "I love it."

"I love *you* Mrs Walker," he murmurs as he kisses

me. I wrap my arms around his neck and melt into him. I love it when he calls me Mrs Walker. I might have been his wife for almost three years, but I never get tired of hearing him call me that. He pulls out of the kiss and rests his forehead on mine. "I'll get our bags from the truck and we can start a fire, maybe try out the hot tub before dinner?" he says raising his eyebrows suggestively.

"Sounds like a plan," I tell him with a wink. As he goes out to the truck I race around the cabin, exploring every room. The bathroom has a huge tub big enough for both of us, as well as a walk-in shower, and I know we are definitely going to be spending time in here. Making my way up the stairs to the bedroom, I find a huge bed sitting against one wall and large rugs cover the wooden floor. Double doors open out onto a small balcony which overlooks the lake. Pushing the doors open I step outside and see Mason emptying the truck. He turns and waves, a happy smile on his face. I wave back as he carries on getting the bags. Looking out over the lake, all I can hear is the sound of the birds chirping and I already know I'm going to love it here.

CHAPTER THREE

Mason

*A*n hour later and dinner is cooking on the stove. Libby seems a little confused as to the amount I'm cooking. I can't blame her, there is far too much for just the two of us. What she doesn't know is that her cousin Savannah is coming for the night with her boyfriend Josh, and their daughter Hope. When I arranged this trip away I was unsure whether she would want to be away from her family at Christmas. Her parents are in the U.K. and couldn't make it over this year. I know how much she misses them. Sav and Josh however, were more than happy to come and spend Christmas Eve with us before heading back to the ranch for Christmas Day. They weren't due for about another hour and a half and I planned on making the most of our time alone.

Turning from the kitchen I see Libby lying on the rug in front of the fire, her kindle in her hand. Crossing the room, I drop down next to her and she looks up at me startled, obviously engrossed in her book. "Hey gorgeous, what are you reading." She doesn't answer me but her cheeks flush red and she quickly turns her kindle off. I laugh. "Another one of your dirty books?" I ask and she swats me gently on the shoulder.

"They aren't dirty. They're romantic!" she exclaims.

"Any of the guys in those books ever made love to their woman in front of an open fire?" I ask her huskily, my eyes dropping to her mouth. She bites down on her lip and shakes her head. "Good," I mutter as my mouth drops to hers and I kiss her hungrily. I bite gently on her bottom lip and she opens up to me, our tongues duelling together. Her warm hands find their way under my t-shirt and goose bumps erupt on my skin where she touches me. I pull out of the kiss and sit up, removing my top along with hers. Dropping my eyes to her chest, I can see her nipples have pebbled and are pushing against the material of her bra. She's panting from our kisses, her eyes full of desire as she stares at me.

"You are so beautiful Libby," I whisper as I remove her bra and lay her down, my body hovering over hers.

Palming one of her breasts I lower my head and suck her nipple into my mouth. Her back arches pushing her breast closer to me, and a moan falls from her lips. As I continue to swirl my tongue over her nipple my other hand traces down her stomach, and my fingers push under the waistband of her yoga pants. Her panties are damp with her arousal and I slip my fingers under the lace, sliding them easily through her wet folds. Circling her clit, her hips raise off the floor and her fingers dig into my shoulder.

"More Mason," she moans and I bite down on her nipple causing her to gasp. Removing my hand from her panties she whimpers and I chuckle as I slide her yoga pants and panties down her legs. Kicking off my jeans I throw them on the sofa.

"Impatient, aren't we?" I tease, taking hold of her ankle and kissing my way up her leg. She's panting again by the time I reach the inside of her thigh, and I bite down gently on her skin before soothing the area with my tongue. Her hips raise and my tongue sweeps through her folds, before gently sucking her clit into my mouth. Her hands are in my hair and she's holding my head between her legs. I gently push a finger inside her, my tongue never letting up on her clit. I can tell that she's close as I add another finger and her breathing increases. Suddenly her legs are twitching and she's shouting my name as she comes against my mouth. Not giving her a chance to recover, I flip her onto her stomach and pull her hips up towards me. Holding my erection, I guide it inside her, groaning against her back as her body pulls me in. I can still feel the last of her orgasm as her sex pulses around me. Thrusting into her she moans again, and I can feel my release building with each movement. Her body is so in tune with mine, she can sense that I'm close and begins to move with me. Once again, her body erupts and shudders as she comes for a second time, and I follow her collapsing onto her back. Our bodies are slick with sweat and I gently slide out of her, pulling her into my arms, her back to my chest.

We lie in front of the fire wrapped in a throw from the sofa. Libby fell asleep pretty much as soon as I pulled her into my arms. I love holding her while she sleeps but knowing that Savannah and Josh will be arriving soon, I gently stroke my fingers up and down her arm, stirring her from her sleep.

"Libby sweetheart, we should get dressed," I say quietly in her ear, my lips kissing along her jawline.

"But you said no clothes, remember?" she says sleepily, her eyes still closed.

I laugh and pull her closer to me. "I remember baby, but you need to get dressed for dinner." I don't want to ruin the surprise, but if she refuses to get dressed I'm going to have to. I tickle her along her ribs and she squeals.

"Mason! Stop!" she begs trying to squirm away from me. I tickle her again and she manages to break free of my hold. Laughing she grabs her clothes and runs up the stairs. My cock twitches at the sight of her running naked through the cabin. If Savannah and Josh weren't coming I'd be keeping her naked all night, but I'm excited to see her face when they arrive.

CHAPTER FOUR

Libby

*L*aughing, I run up the stairs and away from Mason's tickling hands. Catching my reflection in the full-length mirror I take in my messy hair and flushed cheeks. Anyone looking at me now would know exactly how I'd just spent the last hour. Grabbing my hairbrush, I quickly pull it through my tangled hair throwing it up into a messy bun. Just as I'm about to get dressed I hear Mason shouting.

"Baby, there's someone knocking on the door. Can you get it? I'm just checking on the dinner."

"Okay," I shout back, quickly throwing on some clothes, wondering who the hell can be knocking on the door of our remote cabin. I quickly peer through the window but can't see any cars except Mason's truck.

Running downstairs, I pull the door open and squeal with excitement when I see Savannah, Josh and Hope standing on the other side. "Oh my God!" I cry as I pull Savannah in for a hug. "What are you doing here?"

"Surprise!" Savannah shouts and Hope starts laughing and clapping from Josh's arms.

"Hey beautiful girl," I say to Hope as she holds her arms out to me. Taking her from Josh, I hold her close, loving the smell of baby shampoo and soap.

"Merry Christmas, Aunt Libby," Hope says sweetly before burying her face into my neck. I turn to see Mason standing behind me, a smile on his face as he sees Hope snuggled against me.

"Did you arrange this?" I ask him and he nods as he brushes a kiss across my cheek. "Thank you," I whisper, gazing up at him.

"Guys, can we come in? It's freezing out here?" Josh asks, his voice tinged with amusement as he interrupts our moment.

"Yes, of course," I tell him with a chuckle. Stepping away from the door I let them in, noticing that they are carrying overnight bags. "Are you staying with us?" I ask excitedly.

"Yes, just for tonight," Savannah replies as she passes me. "Oh my God! This place is amazing!" she exclaims rushing up the wooden staircase.

"Jeez Mason," I hear Josh mutter. "Can't you just buy your woman jewelry for Christmas instead of this?" he jokes, his hand gesturing around the cabin. "You're making the rest of us look bad."

"Not my problem you're not as romantic as me Miller," Mason replies winking at me.

Ignoring the guys and their banter I carry Hope to the sofa, sitting down with her on my lap. "So, are you excited for Santa Clause, baby girl?" I ask her and she nods.

"He's bringing me a dolly and a stroller," she tells me her face lighting up with excitement.

"Wow, I love dolls. I hope you'll let me play with you." She nods enthusiastically. "I have a present for you, too. It's back at the ranch." She jumps off my lap and claps her hands together. Turning to see Josh in the kitchen, she races toward him.

"Daddy, Daddy! Aunt Libby got me a present," she cries, crashing into his legs. I watch as he picks her up and she throws her arms around his neck.

"Well aren't you a lucky girl," he says, tickling her side. She squeals and wriggles out of his arms.

"Uncle Mason, where's your Christmas tree?" Hope

asks as she looks around the room. Mason kneels down and whispers something in her ear, I watch as her eyes go wide before she starts jumping around with excitement.

"Remember it's a secret," Mason tells her as he holds his hand out for a high five. Hope reaches up and smacks her tiny hand against his. I smile as I watch them. Mason adores Hope, we all do. Savannah never planned to get pregnant, but Hope brought her and Josh together and I've never seen them happier.

"This place is beautiful, Lib," Savannah says as she sits down next to me. Her eyebrows raise when she notices the crumpled throw on the floor in front of the fire. "Getting a little jiggy in front of the fire, were you Lib?" she asks, nudging my shoulder. I feel my cheeks flush and she nods and smiles. "Thought so! Lucky cow!" she exclaims.

"Oh please! You and Josh can't keep your hands off each other," I scoff.

"True!" she concedes. "But sex in front of a log fire, that's hot!"

"Oh, it was!" I tell her with a wink. The conversation comes to an abrupt end as Hope scrambles onto the sofa and sits herself between us.

"Want to color Aunt Libby?" Hope asks sweetly, holding out a princess coloring book.

"Absolutely," I tell her with a grin, and the three of us spend the next half hour coloring while Mason and Josh finish making dinner.

After we've eaten we spend the evening playing with Hope. Her excitement of being at the cabin and Christmas just around the corner keeps her awake until late into the evening. When she finally falls asleep we are all exhausted and decide to call it a night. All four of us are looking forward to spending Christmas Eve together.

CHAPTER FIVE

Mason

I wake up with Libby's body plastered to mine. She slept in just a pair of panties and one of my t-shirts. I slowly trace my hand up her thigh and under her t-shirt, my fingers stroking her back. She begins to stir and lifts her head, her sleepy eyes finding mine.

"Morning," she says, her voice husky from sleep.

"Good morning beautiful," I lower my head to hers and capture her lips with mine. As the kiss becomes heated, I swipe my tongue along her bottom lip, her mouth opening on a moan. Turning her onto her back, I press her body down into the mattress, my arousal pushing against the thin fabric of her panties. She wraps her legs around my back and rocks her hips into mine. My hand goes under her t-shirt, cupping her breast. As I roll her nipple between my fingers, she claws at my back and pants as I kiss down her neck and around her jaw. I'm just about to pull off her t-shirt when I hear footsteps on the stairs and I still.

"Aunt Libby, Uncle Mason wake up! It's Christmas Eve," a little voice shouts from the stairs.

"Shit, it's Hope!" Libby whisper shouts, quickly scrambling from underneath me. I pull the comforter over us just as Hope bounds into the room.

"Come on Uncle Mason, we have to do the surprise," she shouts, jumping up and down.

"What surprise?" Libby asks, glancing between me and Hope.

"It's a secret," Hope says smugly. Making her way around to my side of the bed, she pulls on my arm until I give in and get up, throwing on a t-shirt I let her take my hand.

"Where's Mommy and Daddy Hope?" I ask as she drags me towards the stairs.

"Downstairs. Daddy sent me to wake you up."

"I bet he did," I mutter glancing back at Libby who's laughing as she watches us.

"Right, let's get this surprise set up then." I scoop Hope up and turn back to Lib. "Stay there gorgeous, I'll let you know when you can come down." She nods and Hope cheers as I carry her downstairs.

I find Savannah and Josh in the kitchen making breakfast. "She found you then?" Josh asks, a grin on his face.

"You're a dick!" I exclaim with a smile, covering Hope's ears with my hands.

Holding his hands up, he laughs. "Just preparing you for what's to come when you've got kids of your own."

"You wouldn't change it for the world," I tell him and he shakes his head.

"No way. I love my girls," he says kissing Savannah before reaching out and tickling Hope.

Smiling I pass him Hope. "Right," I say ruffling her hair. "You stay here and I'll be back in a minute with Libby's surprise." She nods her head, her eyes wide with excitement. I smile as I head for the door, knowing that Libby is going to love her surprise. Pulling my boots on I make my way around the back of the cabin. I'd arranged for the owner to hide a Christmas tree in the storage out back. I'd also managed to hide a box of decorations in the truck, and after decorating the tree I planned to roast marshmallows on the open fire.

The tree was beautiful and it looked perfect next to the fireplace. Running up the stairs, I find Libby sitting patiently on the bed. "Ready, sweetheart?" I ask, pulling her into my arms and kissing her lightly on the nose. She nods and I guide her down the stairs, my hand covering her eyes. Standing in front of the tree, I remove my hand and watch as her face lights up when she sees the tree.

"You got us a Christmas tree!" she exclaims throwing her arms around me. "How? Where did it come from?"

"I asked the owner to get me one. I know the one at home isn't very big and we can't spend Christmas here without a tree." The house we lived in on the ranch was small and there really wasn't room for much of a tree so I knew having a big tree to decorate here would make her happy.

"Look Aunt Libby, decorations!" Hope cries, pointing to the large box by her feet.

Catching my eye, she grins. "You've thought of everything. You're amazing you know that?" she says shaking her head as if she can't believe it.

"Hmmmm," I whisper in her ear. "Maybe you could show me just how amazing you think I am later?" I tease, my lips brushing against her neck.

"I think I can manage that," she replies breathlessly.

"You do know we're here right?" Josh asks, his voice tinged with amusement. "If you want us to wait outside…" I see Savannah hit his shoulder and he laughs.

"Leave them alone, they're in love," Savannah tells him.

"Hey! I'm in love, too!" Josh exclaims, pulling Savannah into his arms and kissing her.

"Can we decorate the tree now?" Hope whines and I scoop her up, twirling her around.

"You bet we can, sweetheart. Come on." She giggles and I pass her to Savannah, who's already made a start emptying out the decorations.

"I love you," Libby whispers as she passes me, her fingers tracing down my arm.

"I love you too, baby."

CHAPTER SIX

Libby

Savannah, Hope and I spend the rest of the morning decorating the tree, with Josh and Mason watching from the sofa. They are quick to tell us where they think certain decorations should go, but we ignore them and put them where we want. Hope can only reach a little way up the tree and chooses to put all of the decorations pretty much in one place. When we're done the tree looks a mess, but it's our mess and I love it. I still can't believe the trouble that Mason has gone to, the cabin, the fairy lights and now the Christmas tree. He never fails to amaze me.

All too soon it's time for Savannah, Josh and Hope to head back to the ranch. Hope is so excited for tomorrow.

Savannah is hoping that spending the day at the cabin along with the journey back will have tired her out enough for her to sleep. I'm not so sure. I think the excitement will win.

"Merry Christmas, Sav," I say, pulling her into a hug. "Have a great day tomorrow."

"And you, Lib," she replies, hugging me tightly.

Kneeling down I open my arms to Hope and she comes barrelling into me. "Merry Christmas, princess. Thank you for coming to see us."

"Merry Christmas, Aunt Libby. I hope Santa Clause knows to bring your presents here tonight," she says, her tiny eyebrows pulled together in a frown.

"Don't worry sweetheart, I've made sure he knows that we're here," Mason tells her with a wink, high fiving her as Josh picks her up and carries her to his car.

We wave from the cabin door as they pull away and Mason whispers in my ear. "Alone at last." His warm breath tickling my skin, making me shiver.

"Fancy a dip in the hot tub?" I ask suggestively.

"Definitely!" he exclaims, running to the bathroom and returning with two towels.

"Eager aren't you?" I tease, taking a towel from him.

"To get you naked? Always!"

I laugh and slowly start to strip out of my clothes as he watches me, his eyes roaming my body. Wrapping the towel around myself, I raise my eyebrows at him. "Are you coming?" He nods and quickly removes his clothes before grabbing my hand and pulling me towards the door.

After making love twice in the hot tub, I can barely keep my eyes open. Mason carries me up to bed and I'm wrapped in his arms and asleep before my head hits the pillow.

CHAPTER SEVEN

Mason

Creeping out of bed, I pad downstairs and into the kitchen. Being as quiet as I can, I make pancakes for both of us before putting everything on a tray to take up to Lib. She's stirring as I enter the bedroom and she smiles when she sees me with a tray of food.

"That smells good, I'm starving."

"Merry Christmas, sweetheart," I tell her, putting the tray on the nightstand and leaning down to kiss her.

"Merry Christmas," she whispers, biting down on her lip. "I'm nervous about giving you your present."

"I'm sure I'm going to love it, Lib," I assure her. "Let's

eat and then we can exchange gifts." She nods and sits up, tucking the comforter around her.

Sliding into the bed, I hold out the plate stacked high with pancakes. She takes one, eating it slowly. Glancing at me she reaches under the bed and pulls out a large present.

"Open it," she tells me, bouncing her legs in excitement.

"I thought you were nervous about giving me my gift?" I ask confused.

"This one I think you'll like, it's the other one I'm nervous about."

"I've got more than one?"

"Kind of," she replies cryptically. "Just open it already."

Laughing, I remove the paper and take the lid off the box. Looking inside I see a new cowboy hat and I smile, knowing how much she loves me in my hat. Taking it out I put it on and she smiles.

"Looking hot, babe. Do you like it?" she asks sounding unsure.

"I love it, Lib. Thank you." Leaning over I kiss her softly on her lips. "Time for your present." Opening the drawer of the nightstand I reach inside, pulling out a small box. Handing it to her, she grins at me before ripping off the paper. When she sees the James Avery box she squeals and quickly opens the lid.

"Oh Mason, it's gorgeous!" she exclaims, holding up the charm bracelet that was nestled inside the box.

"I chose those three charms to get you started, but we can add to it for birthdays and special occasions." I watched as she fingers the charms. There was a rose, a book and a heart.

"I love them, they're perfect. Thank you." She brushes her lips against mine and I tangle my hand in her hair as I kiss her. As she pulls out of the kiss I see her bite down on her lip again, nerves evident on her face. I have no idea what she is going to give me, but whatever it is I know that I'm going love it.

She reaches under the bed again, this time putting a much smaller box on the bed. She passes it to me, her fingers lingering on the box before she lets go. Watching her I slowly remove the paper and lift the lid. As my eyes drop to the contents in the box I gasp, my eyes darting back up to hers. She looks terrified.

"Oh my God, Libby!" I exclaim. "Are you...? Am I...?" I pause my heart racing in my chest. "Are we going to have a baby?" She nods and I drop the box containing the pregnancy test, pulling her into my arms. "Why would you be nervous to tell me? Are you...are you not happy about it?"

She nods. "Yes, of course I'm happy about it, but we talked about waiting until we could afford a bigger place, and I'd managed to find a job. I was worried that the timing wasn't right. How will we manage?"

"Libby, the timing is perfect, sweetheart. I want nothing more than to have babies with you. We'll manage just fine." I place my hand on her flat stomach and smile. "I can't believe I'm going to be a Daddy," I say in awe. "How long have you known?"

"Not long, I found out the day you told me you'd booked to come here. I decided to wait until today to tell you." She pauses and drops her eyes. "You're really okay with it? I know it wasn't planned, I must have missed my pill or something."

"Libby, this is the best Christmas present I have ever had. I can't wait to see your belly swollen with our baby. I love you so much, sweetheart."

"I love you, too," she whispers. "Merry Christmas, Mason."

The End

Printed in Great Britain
by Amazon